THE PIRATE JAMBOREE

THE
PIRATE
JAMBOREE

BY MARK TEAGUE

SCHOLASTIC INC.

ISBN 978-0-545-97095-2
10 9 8 7 6 5 4 3 2 1   16 17 18 19 20   Printed in the U.S.A. 08   First printing 2016
The type was set in Caslon Antique. Book design by Charles Kreloff and David Saylor

To Ava

Morning comes. The ships appear
surging o'er the summer sea.
While from their decks, a lusty cheer:
It's time for the pirate jamboree!

Look at them, this scurvy brood!
Rascals of every kind!
Sailing across the neighborhood,
with mischief on their mind!

They crave adventure. They buckle swash.
Danger they won't flee!
These desperados on their way
to the pirate jamboree!

The Johnson brothers are first in line.
Bluebeard, Blackbeard, and Beigebeard, too—
three terrors of the Seven Seas
and each a scoundrel through and through!

Right behind them, Sharktooth Jane—
a clever outlaw, she!
Her ship is fancy, far from plain,
all thanks to piracy!

"Miss Jane"

And look, you lubbers: It's Eye Patch Sue,
with her curving scimitar.
Her parrot wears an eye patch, too,
and mutters curses near and far.

Ahoy! There's Cap'n Gunderboom,
with cannons strewn across his boat.
I wonder where he finds the room.
I wonder how he stays afloat!

And finally, we meet Peg Leg Jones,
adrift upon the salty sea.
Underneath the skull and bones—
his turn to host the jamboree!

Welcome
Pirates!

With grappling hooks, the pirates swoop
from every ship at sea,
while Jones lets loose a welcoming whoop
to start the jamboree!

They bundle over Peg Leg's bed.
Aye! A wrecking crew!
A lampshade lands on Sharktooth's head.
A table topples, too!

Eye Patch plunders Peg Leg's chest.
I wonder, would he mind?
She grabs the things that she likes best
and leaves the rest behind.

And look! There's Cap'n Gunderboom,
with cannons in the hall.
Shooting missiles 'cross the room
to splatter on the wall!

And now the melee's in full swing.
The Johnsons shout and roar,
making a mess of everything
as they tumble o'er the floor!

But what is this? A ship ahoy?
They train their telescopes to see.
"Oh, no!" they cry. "It can't be so.
It really cannot be!"

Alas! The dreaded Mrs. Jones,
in her black-sailed ship of doom!
Ship of terror! Ship of bones!
It's the S.S. *CLEAN YOUR ROOM!*

"Run away!" the pirates cry.
Overboard they flee,
till only Peg Leg lags behind
to face his destiny.

It's evening now. The sky turns gold.
The pirates' time is short.
Dinner and bed now lie ahead
in every quiet port.

Tonight they'll dream of wild deeds,
no more to run away.
Telling themselves that they'll return
to fight another day!

And in the morning, they'll set sail,
their ships once more at sea.
Another day, another tale,
another pirate jamboree!